For Poppy – G.A.

For my dad, love from David – D.W.

Other books by Giles Andreae and David Wojtowycz:

ABC Animal Jamboree

Commotion in the Ocean

Cock-a-doodle-do! Barnyard Hullabaloo

Dinosaurs Galore!

Rumble in the Jungle

tiger tales

an imprint of ME Media, LLC

5 River Road, Suite 128, Wilton, CT 06897

Published in the United States 2012

Originally published in Great Britain 2011

by Orchard Books

a division of Hachette Children's Books

ISBN-13: 978-1-58925-109-0

ISBN-10: 1-58925-109-1

Printed in China

SCP0511

1 3 5 7 9 10 8 6 4 2

For more insight and activities,

visit us at www.tigertalesbooks.com

Bustle in the Bushes

by

Giles Andreae

Illustrated by

David Wojtowycz

tiger tales

At the bottom of your backyard,
You might just hear a sound—
A chirrup from the treetops
Or a scuttle on the ground.

If you step a little closer,
Maybe you can see
A ladybug, a dragonfly,
A beetle or a bee.

The sun is in the sky
And it's a lovely summer's day.
The minibeasts have seen you
And they want to come and play!

Snail

We're famous for slithering slowly,
But wouldn't you also be slow
If you had to carry
Your house on your back
Wherever you wanted to go?

slither

Slug

We're sticky and we're slimy
And we don't have any bones,
So we hang out under flowerpots
And settle under stones.

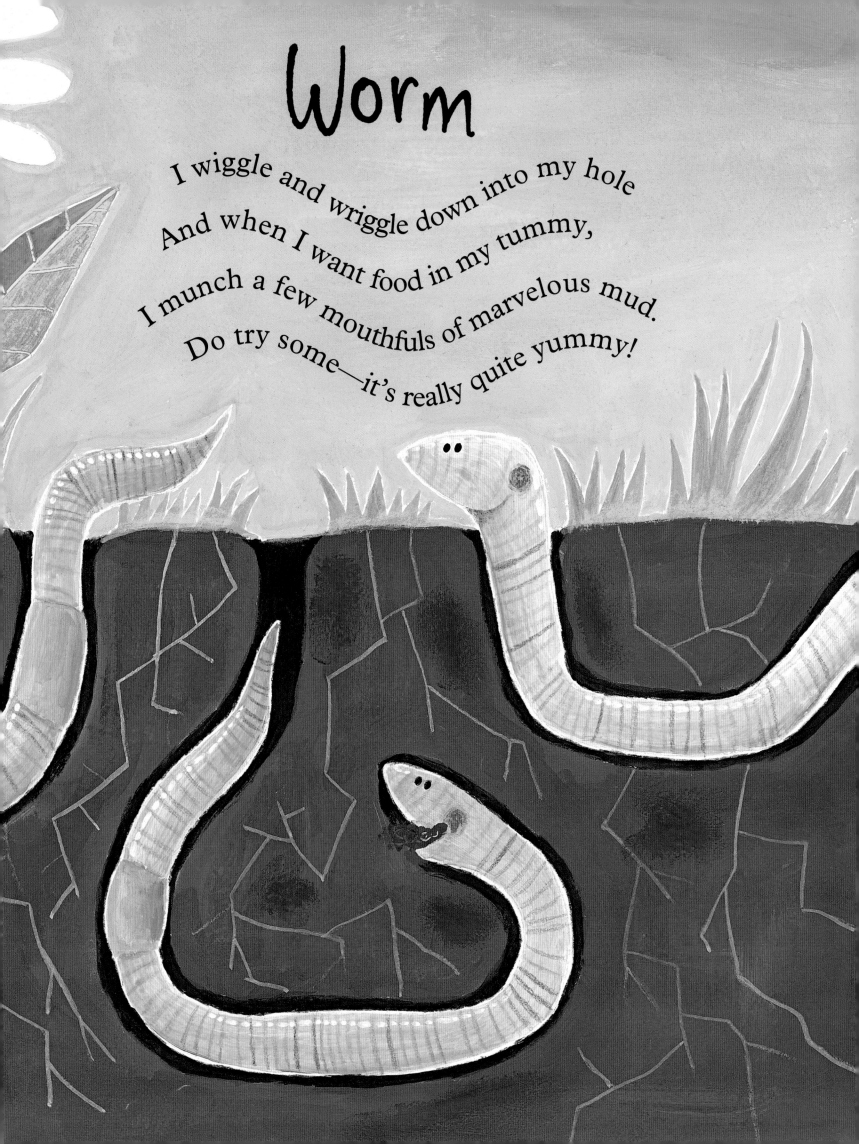

Worm

I wiggle and wriggle down into my hole
And when I want food in my tummy,
I munch a few mouthfuls of marvelous mud.
Do try some—it's really quite yummy!

Spider

I love to wake up in the morning
When my web is all covered with dew.
It's such a fine sight
When it glitters so bright.
Don't you think it's beautiful, too?

Fly

My eyes are big and orange
And my body's black and fuzzy
And I fly around your house all day
Just being very buzzy!

Beetle

We've got these two feelers on top of our heads,
Which wiggle and help us to see,
And we scuttle around
Without making a sound.
Can you scuttle as quickly as me?

Earwig

snip

I like to feed on tasty plants
And trees that have gone rotten.
But the weirdest thing about me
Is these pinchers on my bottom!

Stick Insect

I'd rather not be eaten
So I've got this brilliant trick—
I cling to leaves and branches
And pretend that I'm a stick!

Ant

We ants like to work as an army,
Which means that we do things together.
Just watch how we carry
These leaves to our nest.
You must admit that's pretty clever!

pitter-patter

Caterpillar

I munch on the leaves in the garden.
Then slowly I spin my cocoon.
But now I must sleep
As I'm going to be
A beautiful butterfly soon!

crunch

flutter

Ladybug

How many spots has a ladybug got?

Look at my back and you'll see.

I know that I've got . . .

Well, I've got quite a lot.

Why don't you count them with me?

trot trot trot

Centipede

Hello, I'm the centipede, how do you do?
I'm as friendly as friendly can be.
Now, which of my hands would you
most like to shake?
I've got at least thirty, you see!

Bee

There's nothing that's better than being a bee.
You may think that sounds a bit funny.
But you'd shout "hooray!"
If you lived every day
In a hive full of heavenly honey!

Dragonfly

My wings are like shimmering rainbows
And my body's a dazzling green.
Of all of the animals here in this pond,
Surely I must be the queen!

Grasshopper

We grasshoppers do enjoy jumping
As our legs are incredibly strong.
And when we're not jumping,
We rub them together
To make the most beautiful song.

chirrup

Did you like those minibeasts?
What a lot there are!
Flying, crawling, slithering,
And jumping, oh so far!

Some live by the water
And some live in the air,
Some like living underground
And finding food down there.

But now let's leave the backyard.
We can come another time.
Which beast was your favorite one?
I bet you can't guess mine!